$\neq$
E
G868f

For Catherine Reid

Printed in Italy   10 9 8 7 6 5 4 3 2 1

Library of Congress Cataloging-in-Publication Data   Gretz, Susanna.   Frog in the middle   /   Susanna Gretz.   –   1st American ed.   p.   cm. Summary: Three friends maintain a friendship despite occasional jealousies.   ISBN 0-02-737471-8   [1. Animals – Fiction. 2. Friendship – Fiction. 3. Jealousy – Fiction.] I. Title.   PZ7.G8636Fr   1991   E – dc20 90-3842   CIP   AC

Frog in the Middle

Susanna Gretz

Four Winds Press
New York

Frog, Rabbit, and Duck are friends, but sometimes
Rabbit and Frog won't play with Duck.

So Duck is jealous.

Sometimes Frog and Duck won't play with Rabbit.

So Rabbit is jealous.

Today they are all playing together.
"I'm older than you," Duck tells Rabbit.
"Well, I'm older than Frog," says Rabbit.
"I'm *almost* older," says Frog.

"She's *almost* older!" yells Duck, laughing.

"Almost older!" yells Rabbit, laughing.

"It's my birthday next Sunday. . ." says Frog.

But the other two aren't listening.

On Monday Frog visits Rabbit,

but Duck is too busy to be jealous.
She's making a card.

On Tuesday Frog visits Duck,

but Rabbit is too busy to be jealous.
He's choosing a present.

On Wednesday Duck visits Rabbit.
Frog tries hard not to be jealous.

Rabbit and Duck make a cake.

On Thursday Rabbit and Duck are nowhere to be seen.
"I don't care," Frog says to herself. "I'm going for a swim."

She swims under the water, all the way across the pond.

There are Duck and Rabbit, whispering and giggling together!
Frog is jealous! She swims back to the other side
of the pond and hops sadly home.

Frog is jealous all day Friday. . . all day Saturday. . .

and all Sunday morning.

On Sunday afternoon the doorbell rings.

"SURPRISE!"
It's Duck and Rabbit.

Happy Birthday
FROG
love from
Duck and Rabbit

Everyone has some birthday cake,
and Frog opens her present.

Then they all play together.
First they all play soccer . . .

and then they all play volleyball.

"Let's play waterball," says Duck.
"I can't play that," says Rabbit.
"I'm a *land* animal."

"I *love* waterball," says Duck, diving in.
"But Rabbit can't play waterball," says Frog.

"What did you say?" asks Duck, coming up for air.
"Rabbit can't play waterball," says Frog.
"He's a land animal. He'll be jealous."

Frog and Duck think this over.
"I know what," says Duck. . . .

"Let's play Frog-in-the-Middle!"

And it was the best game ever.